THE RAINBOW BRIDGE

INSPIRED BY A
CHUMASH TALE

RETOLD BY

Audrey Wood

PAINTINGS BY

Robert Florczak

VOYAGER BOOKS

HARCOURT, INC.

San Diego   New York   London

For Louise Howton
—A.W.

For Amy and Lukas
—R. F.

For information about permission to reproduce selections from this book,
write to trade.permissions@hmhco.com or to Permissions, Houghton Mifflin Harcourt Publishing Company,
3 Park Avenue, 19th Floor, New York, New York 10016.

First Voyager Books edition 2000
Voyager Books is a registered trademark of Harcourt, Inc.

The Library of Congress has cataloged the
hardcover edition as follows:
Wood, Audrey.
The rainbow bridge/Audrey Wood;
illustrated by Robert Florczak.
p.   cm.
Summary: A contemporary story based on the
Chumash Indian legend about the origin of dolphins.
1. Chumashan Indians—Legends. 2. Dolphins—Folklore.
[1. Chumashan Indians—Legends. 2. Indians of North
America—Legends. 3. Dolphins—Folklore]
I. Florczak, Robert, ill. II. Title.
E99.C815W66 1995
398.24'52953—dc20   92-17661
ISBN 0-15-265475-5

ISBN 0-15-202106-X pb

LEO 20 19 18 17 16 15 14 13
4500663175

PRINTED IN CHINA

The paintings in this book were hand done in
oil on canvas, sizes 32" x 24" and 32" x 48".
The display type was set in Rudolf Koch.
The text type was set in Goudy Village.
Color separations by Bright Arts, Ltd., Singapore
Printed and bound by LEO, China
Production supervision by Stanley Redfern
Designed by Michael Farmer

Storyteller's Note

FOR THOUSANDS OF YEARS the Chumash Indians occupied an area of the central California coast from what is now Los Angeles northward to San Luis Obispo County. From early times they were a peaceful and artistic people with a distinctive social and spiritual culture.

Their basketry and cave paintings rank among the most outstanding in North America, but their most famous invention was a plank canoe called a *tomol*. This canoe enabled them to travel long distances along the coast and across the Santa Barbara Channel to trade with villagers on the nearby islands. Although fishing was their primary means of sustaining themselves, the Chumash also consumed an abundant variety of plants and animals that flourished in the mild Mediterranean climate extending along the coast and into the verdant valleys and mountains. Unlike many other American Indians, they could obtain all they needed from their natural environment and therefore had no need to raise crops or to domesticate animals.

The Rainbow Bridge was inspired by an oral Chumash Indian legend handed down from generation to generation. I have taken artistic liberty with the original legend by adding characters and expanding the tale into a story form. I wish to thank the staff of the Santa Barbara Museum of Natural History, which generously donated time, attention, and reference materials pertinent to both the writing and illustration of this book.

In Santa Barbara, California, where I reside, the legend of "the rainbow bridge" is still very much alive in the Chumash Indian community. To this day the Chumash Indians honor Hutash and perform a ceremonial dolphin dance. The island known to them as Limuw, forty miles offshore, is now referred to as Santa Cruz Island. When the weather is clear, it is possible to see from the highest mountaintop on Santa Cruz Island to the highest mountaintop on the mainland in Santa Barbara. In the summer dolphins can be seen frolicking and surfing in the waves along the Santa Barbara coast.

The Chumash People: Materials for Teachers and Students provides excellent information for children about the Chumash Indians. For information about ordering the book, write to the Santa Barbara Museum of Natural History, 2559 Puesta Del Sol Road, Santa Barbara, CA 93105 (attention: Education Department).

O N THE ISLAND OF LIMUW, where the heavens touch the sea, Hutash the earth goddess walked alone. The birds and sea lions, flowers and trees all were her friends, but still Hutash was not happy. The earth goddess longed to share her island home with people made in her own image.

When the time was right, Hutash climbed the highest mountain on Limuw and gathered seeds from a sacred plant. Casting the seeds before her, she spoke, "As there are seeds scattered upon the earth, so shall there be people."

The seeds took root within the fertile soil and grew into plants. But when they opened, instead of flowering, people—male and female, young and old—stepped forth. This was the beginning of the Chumash tribe.

The earth goddess was pleased with the people. They were like her children, and she loved them. That night Hutash raised her arms and called to her husband, the Milky Way. "Great wise Sky Snake, behold the Chumash people who are beautiful and strong of limb."

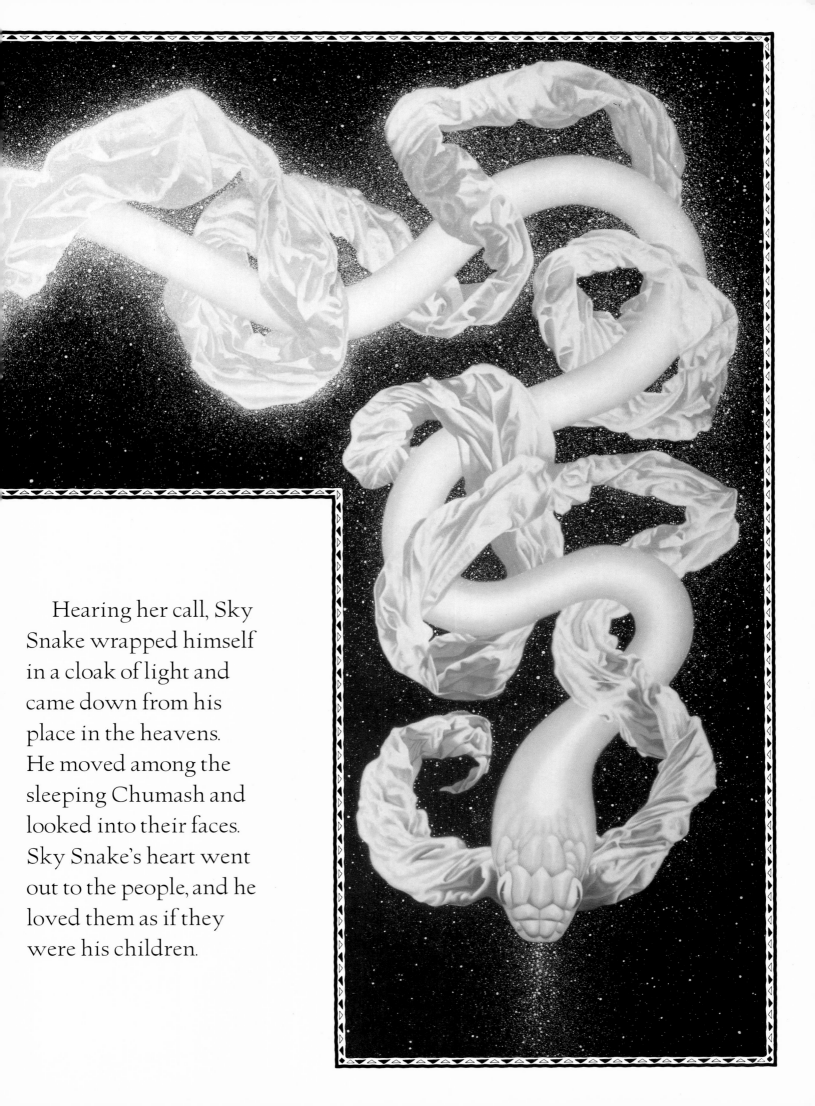

Hearing her call, Sky Snake wrapped himself in a cloak of light and came down from his place in the heavens. He moved among the sleeping Chumash and looked into their faces. Sky Snake's heart went out to the people, and he loved them as if they were his children.

"It is true," he said. "The Chumash are beautiful and strong, but see how they sleep on the cold ground and have no warm food to eat."

Sky Snake returned to his home in the heavens and made a gift for the people. Opening his mouth, he stuck out his tongue and sent a lightning bolt down to Limuw. Where the lightning struck, a fire began to burn.

Awakening from their cold sleep, the Chumash gathered joyfully around the fire. They danced and sang many praises.

In the moons that followed, they learned how to keep the fire burning so that no one was cold at night, and they learned how to cook their food on the glowing embers.

Now the Chumash grew in numbers until the village became busy and crowded.

But once again, Hutash was not happy. Too many children trampled flowers and frightened animals away. Too many mothers cooked on fires and sang to their infants. Too many fathers chanted and danced into the night.

The earth goddess could not sleep. Her eyes were red and swollen, her head throbbed from so much noise. Something had to be done!

Hutash entered the village to talk to the Chumash people, but, one after another, they would not listen. Everyone was too loud and busy.

"*Aiiieeee!*" the goddess cried. "What am I to do?"

In the shade of a hut, a boy and a girl were quietly weaving baskets. The two friends recognized the goddess and saw that she was weary, so they invited her inside.

The girl offered the goddess a bowl of acorn porridge. The boy filled a seashell with springwater and set it before her.

Hutash tasted the porridge, then spoke. "Tell the people that Limuw has grown crowded. In three days, half of you must leave and go to the land across the water; the other half may stay on my island."

Although he was frightened, the boy spoke up. "How can our people cross the ocean? The other land is far away—they will drown."

Hutash finished her porridge, drank the springwater, then wiped her lips. "Tell the people that in three days I will build them a bridge," she said. "Those who have chosen to leave will cross over the water on my bridge."

Without looking back, the goddess left the hut and climbed the highest mountain on Limuw.

When the boy and the girl showed their people the bowl Hutash had eaten from and the seashell from which she had quenched her thirst, the Chumash listened. That day they held a great council and decided who should go to the new land and who should remain on Limuw.

In three days the village awakened to a wondrous
sight. A rainbow bridge stretched from the highest
mountain on Limuw to the highest mountain on the
land across the water.

Soon families began to gather at the bridge. The girl's
family was first in line; the boy's family followed behind.
When it came time to cross over, some of the Chumash were
afraid, so Hutash gave them her blessing.

"Go forth and fill the world with many children,"
she said.

With her blessing in their ears, the people began their
journey across the rainbow.

Halfway over, the boy grew curious. *How can people walk through the sky on such a bridge?* he wondered. Looking down through the rainbow at the rolling waves and the swirling fog, the boy grew dizzy. Although he tried to walk straight, he lost his balance and tumbled off the bridge. As he fell he called out to the girl for help, but she did not hear.

The boy was not alone. Some of the other Chumash also had looked down and were falling into the sea.

On the island of Limuw, the earth goddess heard their cries and saw that they were drowning.

Hutash loved the people and could not bear to lose a single one. With a wave of her hand, the goddess swept away the fog and calmed the sea.

Then she spoke. "As there are people who walk upon the land, so shall there be people who swim in the ocean."

With that Hutash turned the drowning Chumash into dolphins, and they were saved.

As the last person stepped off the bridge onto the new land, the earth goddess pursed her lips and blew into the sky. The rainbow bridge disappeared.

Hutash looked about her and was pleased. Peace and happiness had returned to the island of Limuw.

But all was not well on the new land. At the foot of the bridge the girl waited in vain for her friend. When the rainbow bridge disappeared, she knew he had fallen into the ocean, and she feared he was drowning.

Bitter tears fell from the girl's eyes as she ran down the mountain, across the beach, and dove into the sea. She called out to her friend, hoping he would hear, but the boy was nowhere in sight.

Then, from all sides, rising out of the waves, dolphins—male and female, young and old— surrounded the swimming girl. Jumping into the air, the dolphins called to each other in their whistling voices.

One young dolphin boldly swam closer than all the rest. The girl looked into its dark eyes and was not afraid. She encircled its neck with her arms. Her sadness disappeared, for the girl understood then what the Chumash understand to this day—the dolphins of the sea are brothers and sisters of their tribe.

A NICE WALK IN THE JUNGLE

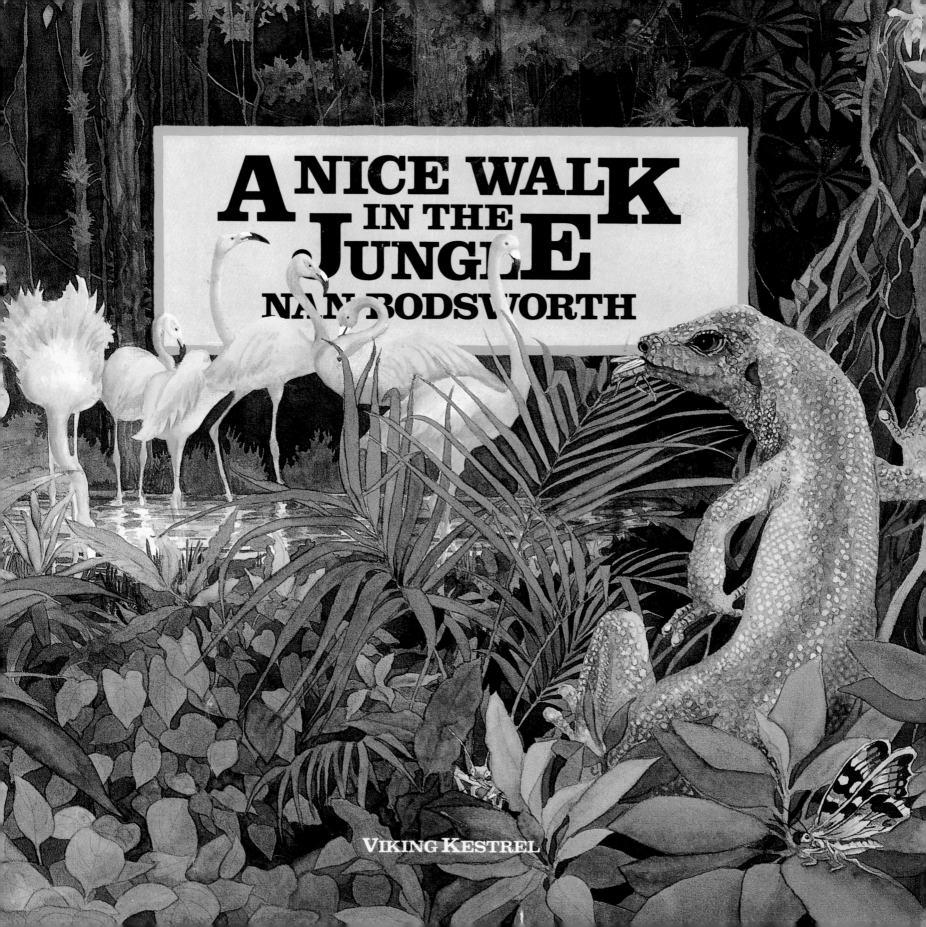

A NICE WALK IN THE JUNGLE

NAN BODSWORTH

VIKING KESTREL

Dedicated to Kim Anderson

For all absent-minded parents and
enthusiastic teachers

———————

Viking Kestrel
Penguin Books Australia Ltd
487 Maroondah Highway, P.O. Box 257 Ringwood, Victoria 3134, Australia
Penguin Books Ltd, Harmondsworth, Middlesex, England
Viking Penguin Inc., 40 West 23rd Street, New York, N.Y., 10011 U.S.A.
Penguin Books Canada Limited, 2801 John Street, Markham, Ontario, Canada L3R IB4
Penguin Books (N.Z.) Ltd, 182-190 Wairau Road, Auckland 10, New Zealand

First published by Penguin Books Australia Ltd 1989

Copyright © Nan Bodsworth, 1989

Produced by Viking O'Neil
56 Claremont Street, South Yarra, Victoria 3141, Australia
A division of Penguin Books Australia Ltd

Designed by John Nicholson
Typeset in Plantin by Trade Graphics Pty Ltd, Melbourne
Printed and bound in Hong Kong through Bookbuilders Limited

National Library of Australia
Cataloguing-in-Publication data

Bodsworth, Nan, 1936 -
A nice walk in the jungle.
ISBN 0 670 82476 3.

1. Jungle ecology — Juvenile literature.
2. Jungle fauna — Juvenile literature.
I. Title.

574.5'2642

'Good morning, Class,' Miss Jellaby said.
'Line up please, and listen to me!
It's Nature Study Day today, and we're all going
for a nice walk in the jungle.'

So, two by two, Miss Jellaby's class lined up —
  Tim and Maria
  Peter and Jim
  Mai Linh and Penny
  Jake and Jenny
  Paul and Tony
  and Melanie and Kim —
and walked out through the school gate and
into the jungle.

'Now, Class, pay attention!' said Miss Jellaby.
'We'll be perfectly safe if we stay on the path.
This is our Nature Walk, so look about you.
If you see something exciting, tell me,
and then I can point it out to everyone.'

Tim saw that they were being followed
by a boa constrictor.
'Miss…' he cried.

But Miss Jellaby wasn't listening.

Miss Jellaby said, 'Ooh! Look, Class!
Look up high in that tree!
There's a furry black spider that's just caught a fly!
What wonderful things we can see in the jungle!'

'Please, Miss...' cried Tim.

'Not now, Tim!' said Miss Jellaby.

Miss Jellaby said, 'Goodness, Class!
Look down here on the grass!
Watch the ants as they drag this beetle away!
What a dangerous place the jungle can be!'

'Please, Miss Jellaby...' cried Tim.

'Just a minute, dear!'

Miss Jellaby said, 'Gracious, Class!
Look under these rocks!
Did you see the lizard snap up that cricket?
You need to be quick to survive in the jungle!'

'Oh please, Miss Jellaby...' cried Tim.

'Wait for your turn, Tim!'

Miss Jellaby said, 'Gather round, Class,
and look into this plant!
See how the caterpillar has fallen inside!
Nothing is safe out here in the jungle!'

'Oh please, Miss Jellaby, look...' cried Tim.

'Tim, dear, don't interrupt!'

Miss Jellaby said, 'Come over here, Class,
and watch the little fish swimming in the pool!
Do you think they're piranhas?
We should look them up when we get back to school!'

'Ooh, *please*, Miss Jellaby, listen to me…!' cried Tim.
'That big snake's swallowed Peter, Maria and Jim,
Mai Linh and Penny, Jake and Jenny, Paul and Tony,
and Melanie and Kim! I'm the only one left!'

'Yes, dear. I'm listening, Tim,' said Miss Jellaby.

Miss Jellaby said, 'Come closer, Class!
If you stand on tiptoe, and look over this log,
you will see a most beautiful yellow tree frog...

Tim! Stop pulling at me!'

'H-E-L-P!' cried Tim.

'What did you say, dear?'

Then Miss Jellaby turned around...
and she saw the great, fat, lumpy boa constrictor
lying on the jungle path.

'What are you doing here?' she cried.
'And WHERE'S my class?'

The boa constrictor just burped.

'How DARE you eat my class!'
cried Miss Jellaby.

And she punched that enormous, bumpy boa constrictor
right on his tender nose.

Then she picked up the wobbly boa by his scaly tail
and shook and shook...

And out came Tim and...

...Peter and his wheelchair
Maria and Jim
Mai Linh and Penny
Jake and Jenny
Paul and Tony
and Melanie and Kim.

Miss Jellaby counted her class twice
to make sure they were all there.
Then she took that thin, grumpy boa constrictor,
and wound him round and round a jungle tree,
and tied him in a big knot!
'*That* will teach you to eat my class!' she said.

Which reminded her that it was lunch time.
'There's bound to be a Burger Bungalow near here,' she said.
'Anywhere in the world, they're never far away.'

And sure enough, around the corner
was a Burger Bungalow.
'It says HERBIVORES on one door,
and CARNIVORES on the other,' said Tim.
'What does that mean?'

'Well, Tim,' said Miss Jellaby,
'herbivores eat plants, and carnivores eat meat.
I think we've met enough meat eaters today,
so we'll have lunch with the herbivores.'

'Now,' said Miss Jellaby, 'where shall
we go for next week's Nature Walk?'
'Let's go to the zoo!' said Tim.